This SCRIBBLERS
book belongs to:

....

This edition published in Great Britain in MMXIX
by Scribblers, an imprint of
The Salariya Book Company Ltd
25 Marlborough Place,
Brighton BN1 1UB
www.salariya.com

SCRIBO BOOK HOUSE SCRIBBLERS

© The Salariya Book Company Ltd MMXIX
Text & Illustrations © Dorien Brouwers MMXIX

HB ISBN-13: 978-1-912537-25-9

1 3 5 7 9 8 6 4 2

A CIP catalogue record for this book is
available from the British Library.

Printed and bound in China

Printed on paper from sustainable sources

Visit
www.salariya.com
for our online catalogue and
free fun stuff.

FOR WILLIAM
a remarkable little being

THE REMARKABLE PIGEON

DORIEN BROUWERS

SCRIBBLERS
a SALARIYA *imprint*

One sunny day a pigeon landed in the zoo.

It decided to visit all the bird cages.

'What a wonderfully big beak the toucan has...
I wish mine wasn't so tiny!'

'And look at the size of the ostriches.
Even their babies are bigger than me.
I feel so small!'

The pigeon watched the
hummingbirds flying backwards.
'Gosh, that's clever,' it thought,
'I can only fly forwards.'

'Wow, eagles are
so strong and
handsome. They
make me feel weak.'

'How can flamingos balance on one leg for such a long time? I'd just wobble and fall over.'

'I'd love to be as colourful as a parrot.
Why am I so plain and grey?'

The pigeon started to feel sad.
It didn't seem to be very good at
anything and it felt... rather boring.

The pigeon was so glum that
it didn't even notice all the
beauty of the world around it.
It walked on...

'Just look at how fast the penguins can swim.
I am very clumsy in the water.'

'And look, the heron can swallow a whole fish at once! Pigeons only peck at scraps and crumbs.'

'Oh... listen to the songbirds singing.
If only my cooing could sound so sweet.'

'Owls are so clever. They can
stay awake all night long,'
the pigeon sighed.

But seeing the wise owl made
the pigeon think...

The pigeon puffed up its chest.
'It's okay to be me,' it cooed. 'I'm
remarkable because, look...'

'I'm free and I can fly away!'

So, the remarkable pigeon flew all around the world and had lots of incredible adventures.

PICTURE GLOSSARY

HUMMINGBIRD

There are more than 340 different varieties of hummingbird. They are found only in the Americas, mainly South America. The hummingbird is the smallest species of bird in the world. They are fast flyers and some can flap their wings as fast as 200 times per second. As well as flying forwards they can also hover, fly backwards, sideways and even upside down! They love to dip their long tongues into flowers to suck up the nectar for energy. Sometimes they will eat small insects and spiders as a little snack.

TOUCAN

Toucans live in the forests of South America, in
small flocks of five to six birds. They have wonderful,
brightly-coloured bills, which are large in comparison
to the size of their body. Their bill might look heavy
but it's actually really light so they can easily peel fruit,
which is their main source of food. They also enjoy the
occasional insect, reptile or egg. Toucans aren't very
good at flying and prefer to hop from tree to tree.

OSTRICH

Ostriches live in Africa in herds of up to 12. They
are the world's heaviest and largest species of bird.
Unsurprisingly, they also lay the world's largest eggs. An
ostrich's brain is very small. In fact, its eye is bigger than
its brain. Unlike other birds, ostriches cannot fly, but with
their strong legs they can run very fast, reaching speeds
of up to 70 kph (43 mph). Male and female birds have
different colours: males are black with a white tail, while
females are mostly brown. They feed on flowers, plants,
seeds and even lizards and insects.

FLAMINGO

Flamingos are found all around the world, from the Caribbean and South America to Africa, the Middle East and Europe. There are only six different species of flamingo. They love to be part of a huge flock called a flamboyance. They are great flyers and also enjoy wading in water. While in the water they stir up mud with their feet. They scoop up the muddy water with their beaks and drain it, so they can eat the algae, crustaceans, molluscs, worms and insects that are left behind. In fact, their pink colour is caused by a pigment found in their food.

PARROT

Parrots are mostly found in tropical and subtropical regions of the world. They live in large flocks of up to twenty or thirty birds. There are about 390 species. They come in many different colours and sizes, and can live for a very long time. Most parrots feed on nuts and seeds but some eat fruit, flowers and small insects. Parrots are intelligent birds who are very good at copying sounds they hear in their environment. Some can even talk like humans.

EAGLE

Eagles are very large and powerful birds of prey.
There are over 60 different species of eagle and they
mainly live in Africa, Eurasia, America and Australia.
Eagles have very good eyesight. They can see more
colours and up to eight times further than humans
can. These clever birds love to hunt and use their
strong claws, called talons, to catch prey. Some species
like to eat fish while others prefer rabbits, squirrels,
snakes and small birds. Some eagles can catch even
bigger animals like goats, monkeys and deer.

Owl

There are about 200 different varieties of owl, found all over the world from deserts to forests. These birds of prey are nocturnal, which means they are mostly active at night. With their big eyes owls can see very well in the dark. They are silent fliers who hunt at night for mice, lizards and other small creatures. Like eagles they use their strong talons to catch prey. They can't move their eyes so they must turn their head to see in different directions. Some owls can turn their head almost completely around.

Songbird

Songbirds are known for their beautiful singing. People love to hear them sing and each species has a different song. Songbirds talk to each other by using their different pitches and rhythms. They practise a lot to get their song just right. There are thousands of different songbird species living all over the world. Many songbirds are grey or brown, but some have vibrant coloured feathers like red, blue and even purple. They mainly live on insects and can eat as many as 300 a day, but they also enjoy fruit, nuts and seeds.

PENGUIN

Penguins can't fly. Instead they spend most of their time underwater trying to catch fish, squid, crab and other sea-life. With their streamlined bodies and powerful flippers, they are fast swimmers and can dive to depths of over 250 metres (820 feet). Their black and white feathers give them excellent camouflage while swimming. Penguins can stay underwater for 15 minutes before surfacing for air. There are 17 different species of penguin, mainly found in the Southern Hemisphere. They live in large colonies numbering tens of thousands.

HERON

It's easy to recognise a heron by its elongated, s-shaped neck, long legs and sharp, pointed bill. Herons can be found in almost every country except for Antarctica. They love to eat fish, but also eat frogs, reptiles, insects and even small mammals and birds. There are over 64 different species of heron, some big, some small. Depending on the species, they can be black, brown, white or grey. Herons live near lakes, rivers and wetland as well as by the ocean. Some migrate south every year to avoid cold winter temperatures.

PIGEON

Pigeons come in different colours and sizes. They can fly incredibly fast. Racing pigeons can fly as fast as 145 kph (90 mph). Pigeons are also excellent navigators and always find their way home. Humans have used carrier pigeons to pass messages to each other. They are intelligent, social birds who can even recognise the human alphabet and themselves in a mirror, which is something very few animals can do. Pigeons live in nearly every city in the world. They are so common that we often overlook them. Let's not forget how remarkable they really are!